To

....

With love from

....

For
my mum
– S.W.

Published in Great Britain in 2002 by Gullane Children's Books
This paperback edition published in 2002 by

GULLANE
CHILDREN'S BOOKS

Winchester House,
259-269 Old Marylebone Road, London, NW1 5XJ
First published as *Angel's Christmas Cookies* in the USA in 2002
by HarperCollins Children's Books, a division of HarperCollins Publishers, Inc.

1 3 5 7 9 10 8 6 4 2

A CIP record for this title is available from the British Library.

ISBN 1 86233 452 8 hb
ISBN 1 86233 428 5 pb

Printed and bound China

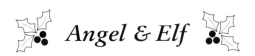

Angel & Elf

C   ar

Angel & Elf

Christmas Bear

Sam Williams

GULLANE
CHILDREN'S BOOKS

Angel and Elf were in Elf's kitchen making
Angel's special recipe – Christmas cookies.
They were also making a big mess!
The air was filled with cinnamon and nutmeg.

While the cookies baked in the oven,
Angel and Elf watched the snow falling gently outside,
but they forgot all about the cookies.

Too late . . . the cookies were burnt.
"Oh dear," said Elf. "What a waste."
"Never mind," said Angel. "I have an idea."

Angel threaded ribbons through each of
the cookies and made a loop at the top.

Elf added some icing.

Then, Angel and Elf popped the cookies into a little
box and set off to see their friend Christmas Tree.

"Hello, Christmas Tree," called Angel and Elf.

"Hello," said Christmas Tree, her lights twinkling.

"We've brought you a gift," said Angel and Elf,
and they offered the box to Christmas Tree.

"Hmmmm, Angel's Christmas cookies!" she said.
"Oh, how lovely. Thank you! They're wonderful!"
Angel and Elf carefully placed the cookies
on Christmas Tree's snowy branches.

"How do I look?" asked Christmas Tree.
"Good enough to eat!" joked Angel and Elf.
They stayed a while and chatted, but soon it
was time for bed. The friends waved goodbye.
The smell of the cookies drifted through the air.

That night, Christmas Tree heard
loud scrunchy, crunchy footsteps
coming towards her in the snow.
Suddenly, a huge baby snowbear appeared.
"Schniffly sniff," said the baby snowbear,
sniffing Christmas Tree's new cookies.
"Schoo!" said Christmas Tree. "Go away!"

"Baby love cookies and big sparkly,"
said the snowbear and grabbed some of
the cookies, dancing off into the night.
"Help!" called Christmas Tree.

Then, Christmas Tree realised the snowbear had taken her special Christmas star as well as her cookies.

The next morning, Angel and Elf went to visit Christmas Tree again. She was very upset.

Christmas Tree told them her sad story.

"My wonderful Christmas star," she sobbed.

"How will I ever get it back?"

"Poor Christmas Tree," said Elf.

"I'm sure we can help you somehow."

"Don't worry," said Angel as she waved her magic wand.
A moment later, Blitzen, one of Santa's fastest reindeer,
flew in at great speed.

"You've got one cookie left, Christmas Tree,"
said Angel. "May I take it?"
"Of course," replied Christmas Tree.

"Come on, Elf," said Angel.
"We'll see you later, Christmas Tree."
Angel, Elf and Blitzen took flight for the
Snowdome Mountains . . . giant snowbear country.

Blitzen landed gently near the snowbears' cave.

A huge white fluffy baby snowbear appeared.
"Lickle peeple," giggled the creature,
its big eyes looking playful.

Angel, Elf and Blitzen stared in amazement.

They had never seen a snowbear before.

"If that's a baby," said Elf, "how big is Mum?"

They were about to find out!

The ground shivered, quivered and shook!
Then, the baby snowbear's mum appeared.
She was gigantic!

Angel flew up to the snowbears.

The baby cuddled its mum tightly.

Angel said hello and introduced herself.

She explained to the big mother snowbear

what had happened to Christmas Tree's star.

The snowbear's mum looked at her baby.
"Do you have Christmas Tree's star, baby?"
The baby snowbear cuddled even closer to
Mum and tightened one of its paws.
"Baby," said Mum, slowly and softly.
"Show me what you have in your paw."

"Baby find," whispered the baby. "Baby keep."
"But it belongs to Christmas Tree," said Mum.
The snowbear baby hunched its shoulders
and uncurled its big fluffy paw.
There was Christmas Tree's star.
The baby snowbear looked very sad.

Angel held out the cookie she had
taken from Christmas Tree.
"Could we swop?" asked Angel.
The baby snowbear's eyes lit up.
Mum gave an approving glance.

Angel gave the big baby a Christmas cookie in exchange
for the star, but Angel could see that the cookie
was far too small for this big baby.

So, with one magical wave of Angel's wand, the
tiny Christmas cookie became a giant Christmas cookie!

"I'm so sorry," said the snowbear's mum.

"Me sorry, too," said the baby snowbear.

Angel smiled, and they said their goodbyes.

They waved to the snowbears, and the snowbears
waved back as Angel, Elf and Blitzen flew away.

Christmas Tree was so pleased to see Blitzen
and her little friends returning safely.
The carol singers had come to see what
all the excitement was about.

Angel put Christmas Tree's star in its rightful place.
Christmas Tree thanked them all.
"Would you like Angel to make you some
more cookies?" asked Elf.
"No, thank you, Elf," Christmas Tree replied
politely. "They smell *too* delicious!"

Everyone laughed and the carol singers, who had
a song for every occasion, began to sing:

*"Oh, what a won-der-ful
thing to be,
a glor-i-ous,
spark-ling
Christ-mas Tree."*

Merry
Christmas,
everyone!

Other Gullane Children's Books
for you to enjoy

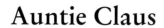

Auntie Claus

Elise Primavera

Harry and the Snow King

Ian Whybrow • Adrian Reynolds

The Sorcerer's Apprentice

Sally Grindley • Thomas Taylor

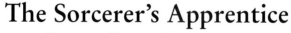

The Snow Friends

Ian Whybrow • Tiphanie Beeke